Copyright © 2023 by Puppy Dogs & Ice Cream, Inc.
All rights reserved. Published in the United States
by Puppy Dogs & Ice Cream, Inc.

ISBN: 978-1-957922-93-5
Edition: March 2023

PDIC and Puppy Dogs & Ice Cream are trademarks
of Puppy Dogs & Ice Cream, Inc.

For all inquiries, please contact us at:
info@puppysmiles.org

To see more of our books, visit us at:
www.PuppyDogsAndIceCream.com

To my mom Aiping:
Your love, dedication and
sacrifices paved the path
for me to grow and
find myself, and continue
to shape me every day.
I love you.

Nurturing Our Sadness
by Dr. Ying Wang, MD

Have you ever felt like curling up into a ball and crying? Perhaps when you had to say goodbye to someone you love? Or when things didn't turn out the way you had hoped, even though you tried your very best?

That feeling is called sadness – it happens when we are unhappy, upset, or down. Sadness can feel like a lump in your throat, an achy heart, or an invisible cloud hanging over your head, making everything dark and gloomy. Sadness is a normal part of life and can even be valuable! It can help us work through difficulties and make positive changes. It can make us appreciate the good things we have, and become more compassionate towards others who are suffering. But too much sadness can leave us feeling exhausted and hopeless. It can even impact how we eat, play, learn and sleep.

The key is to not avoid feelings of sadness, but to recognize, understand, and use it in healthy ways. Here are my suggestions:

First, we remind ourselves that sadness is OK to have. It does not mean weakness or failure. It is something everyone feels, and it will not last forever. Like many other feelings, it is a part of life, and it too, shall pass.

Second, we put feelings into words. Find someone you trust and talk it through. If you prefer to write or draw — that is perfectly fine too. Turning sadness into words (or pictures) takes away its power and makes us feel less stuck. Describe in detail the sadness you feel, point out where in your body that sadness lives, and try to figure out why you may be feeling this way. Occasionally, sadness seems to come out of nowhere. By talking it through, we have a better chance of figuring out what is really going on. With more understanding, we feel more in control, and are more able to come up with solutions.

Sometimes, our sadness is just too much and we don't have the words. In that situation, we move to the third step, taking care of our bodies. Do something that makes your body relax and feel good: take a warm bath, cuddle up with a plushie in a cozy corner, or ask for hugs and kisses from someone you love. Alternatively, you could get moving: jump, run, hop, or dance! Physical activities release feel-good chemicals that boost your mood. If we feel good in our bodies, our emotions and our thoughts will follow suit.

Sometimes, no amount of relaxation or movement is enough, and we really just need a good cry. In that case, let the tears roll.

Finally, know that there is always help. There are professionals who can help you get better at managing your sadness — ask a trusted adult to help you find one. It can make a big difference.

Next time you feel sad, come back to these pages to remind yourself: sadness is OK to have. It may even be useful. You don't need to run away from feelings — you have the tools to cope with them in a healthy way!

Simon was a monkey,
He lived up in a tree.
One day he woke up crying,
As sad as he could be.

The sun was brightly shining,
Bananas tasted fine.
The bumble bees were buzzing,
The honey was divine.

Simon felt all funny,
His funky feeling grew.
Inside, his tummy twisted,
Outside, his face seemed blue.

Simon ate his breakfast, Toucan hummed a song.
Simon sat in silence, his friend asked, "What is wrong?"

"Have some flies or something!" Tree frog blew a kiss.
Snake said "Sssssun is soothing, a sun nap is pure blissss."

Elephant sprayed Simon,
But didn't stop his pout.
"Mud baths are refreshing,
They always help me out!"

Tiger took him racing,
"It makes me feel so free!"
But Simon still felt blue inside,
As sad as he could be.

Nothing helped to lift his mood,
Poor Simon just felt sad.

Knowing they all tried to help,
Simon just felt bad.

"Stop with this attention,
I've told you all along...

No muddy baths, or crunchy snacks,
You hear me? Nothing's wrong!"

"No one needs to help me out,
I'd like to be alone!"

Simon stomped off through vines,
And went out on his own.

Simon soon untangled,
All the branches from Sloth's hair.
"Sloths move so deliberately,
How did you get tangled there?"

"Most sloth days pass by peacefully,
No stress up off the ground.
Today, I just felt out of sorts,
Like life was upside down."

"We have to hold on very tight,
Our claws need certain grip.
So, when I lost my train of thought,
My grasp began to slip."

Simon helped the stranded sloth,
Grab back on his old tree.
"Today I'm feeling upside down,
Could you, perhaps, help me?"

"Monkey, we are animals,
Not robots made of gears.
Emotions are part of life,
We all have hopes and fears.

Yesterday, it rained a lot,
It soaked me through and through.
The sun is shining bright again,
Today, the sky is new."

"When it rains, I fill my cup,
Perhaps I shower off.
Rainstorms have a purpose, too,
Even for a sloth.

If you're feeling blue today,
Think of it like rain.
Emotions all have meaning,
Like a storm within your brain."

"Sometimes," Simon then replied,
"I lose my balance, too.
I've fallen from my treetop home,
And wound up stuck, like you.

Here I was to help you out,
To lift you back up there.
I guess I need to ask for help,
I know my friends all care."

"That prickly brush sure held me tight,
I couldn't move an inch!

Were I alone, I'd tangle more,
The thorns would poke and pinch.

Sadness is a prickly brush,
Sometimes we need a hand,

It's okay to ask for help,
Your friends will understand."

The sloth moved slowly through the tree,
And Simon said "Goodbye."
"Some days, we all have thunderstorms,
Some days, monkeys cry.

Not every day will bring monsoons,
But jungles need the rain.
Without it, forests wouldn't grow,
Our lives would be so plain."

I don't have one emotion,
I'm like the jungle, too.

Some days, I may feel bright inside,
And some days, I feel blue.

On certain days, I need a hand,
Like the sloth I helped today.

I'll tell my friends, "This monkey's sad!
I promise, that's OK."

All emotions have a purpose,
Like the weather in the sky.
Feelings pass with time and talk,
Sometimes, there is no "why."

No emotion lasts forever,
Your rainbow will soon appear.
Don't let sadness hide your shine,
Better days are always near.!

CPSIA information can be obtained
at www.ICGtesting.com
Printed in the USA
JSHW041045020523
41132JS00009B/53